Animals That Live in the Desert

Coyotes

JoAnn Early Macken

Reading consultant: Susan Nations, M. Ed.,
author, literacy coach, consultant

Please visit our web site at: www.earlyliteracy.cc
For a free color catalog describing Weekly Reader® Early Learning Library's list of high-quality books, call 1-877-445-5824 (USA) or 1-800-387-3178 (Canada). Weekly Reader® Early Learning Library's fax: (414) 336-0164.

Library of Congress Cataloging-in-Publication Data

Macken, JoAnn Early, 1953-
Coyotes / JoAnn Early Macken.
p. cm. – (Animals that live in the desert)
Includes bibliographical references and index.
ISBN 0-8368-4826-8 (lib. bdg.)
ISBN 0-8368-4833-0 (softcover)
1. Coyote–Juvenile literature. I. Title.
QL737.C22M34 2005
599.77'25–dc22 2005042268

This edition first published in 2006 by
Weekly Reader® Early Learning Library
A Member of the WRC Media Family of Companies
330 West Olive Street, Suite 100
Milwaukee, WI 53212 USA

Art direction: Tammy West
Cover design and page layout: Kami Koenig
Picture research: Diane Laska-Swanke

Picture credits: Cover, © Gerald & Buff Corsi/Visuals Unlimited; p. 5 © Barbara Gerlach/Visuals Unlimited; pp. 7, 19 © Michael H. Francis; p. 9 © Tom and Pat Leeson; pp. 11, 15 © Steven Holt/Stockpix.com; p. 13 © Elizabeth Delaney/Visuals Unlimited; p. 17 © Richard Day/Daybreak Imagery; p. 21 © Charlie Heidecker/Visuals Unlimited

Printed in the United States of America

1 2 3 4 5 6 7 8 9 09 08 07 06 05

Note to Educators and Parents

Reading is such an exciting adventure for young children! They are beginning to integrate their oral language skills with written language. To encourage children along the path to early literacy, books must be colorful, engaging, and interesting; they should invite the young reader to explore both the print and the pictures.

Animals That Live in the Desert is a new series designed to help children read about creatures that make their homes in dry places. Each book explains where a different desert animal lives, what it eats, and how it adapts to its arid environment.

Each book is specially designed to support the young reader in the reading process. The familiar topics are appealing to young children and invite them to read – and reread – again and again. The full-color photographs and enhanced text further support the student during the reading process.

In addition to serving as wonderful picture books in schools, libraries, homes, and other places where children learn to love reading, these books are specifically intended to be read within an instructional guided reading group. This small group setting allows beginning readers to work with a fluent adult model as they make meaning from the text. After children develop fluency with the text and content, the book can be read independently. Children and adults alike will find these books supportive, engaging, and fun!

– Susan Nations, M.Ed., author, literacy coach,
and consultant in literacy development

A coyote is a wild dog. Coyotes are bigger than foxes. Coyotes are smaller than wolves.

Most coyotes are gray or brown. Some coyotes live in the desert. Their fur is a lighter color. Light colors help them stay cooler.

Coyotes have bushy tails and long legs. They can run fast. They can trot for hours.

tail

legs

Coyotes have large, pointed ears. They can hear well. They can hear other animals moving.

ears

Baby coyotes are called **pups**. Their mother feeds them milk at first. They live in a den for about two months.

pups

Their father guards the den. When the pups come out, he teaches them to hunt. They hunt at night. The desert is cooler at night.

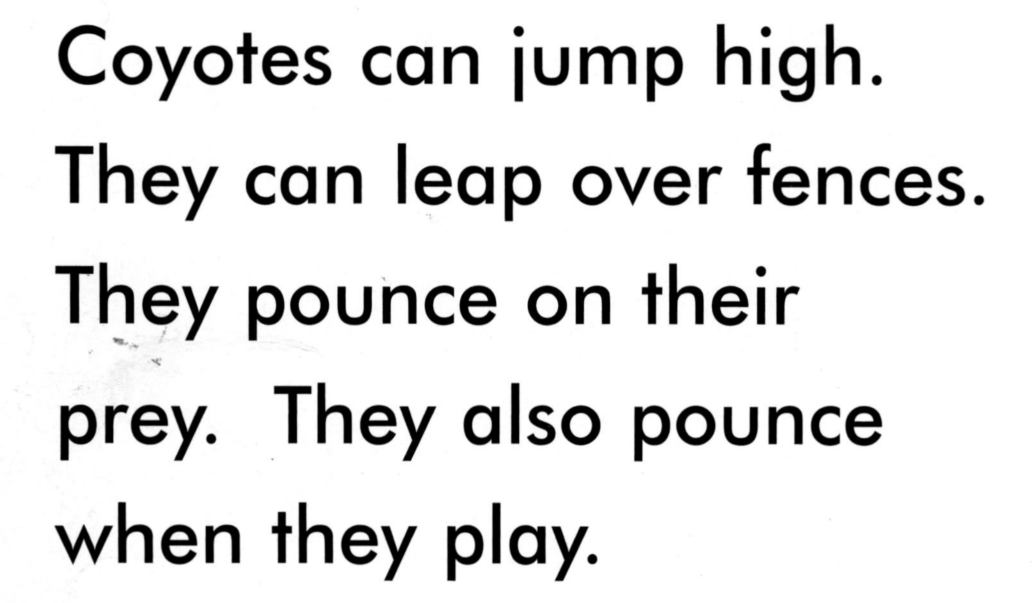

Coyotes can jump high. They can leap over fences. They pounce on their prey. They also pounce when they play.

Coyotes hunt rabbits, mice, lizards, and snakes. They eat nuts and fruit. They eat dead animals they find.

Coyotes can be noisy. They howl and bark. They yip and yelp. They call across the desert.

GLOSSARY

den — a place where a wild animal rests or lives

desert — a very dry place

guards — keeps watch over, protects

leap — to jump

pounce — to jump on

prey — an animal that another animal eats

FOR MORE INFORMATION

BOOKS

Coyotes. Grassland Animals (series). Patricia J. Murphy (Capstone Press)

Coyotes. Welcome to the World of Animals (series). Diane Swanson (Gareth Stevens)

Foxes and Their Homes. Animal Habitats (series). Deborah Chase Gibson (PowerKids Press)

Wolves. Scholastic Science Readers (series). Carolyn B. Otto (Scholastic)

WEB SITE

Creature Feature: Coyotes
www.nationalgeographic.com/kids/creature_feature/0005/
Fun facts, a map, a postcard, and more

About the Author

JoAnn Early Macken is the author of two rhyming picture books, *Sing-Along Song* and *Cats on Judy*, and many other nonfiction books for beginning readers. Her poems have appeared in several children's magazines. A graduate of the M.F.A. in Writing for Children and Young Adults program at Vermont College, she lives in Wisconsin with her husband and their two sons. Visit her Web site at www.joannmacken.com.